ANDERSON ELEMENTARY SCHOOL LIBRARY

Inside the NFL

THE
CAROLINA
PANTHERS

BOB ITALIA
ABDO & Daughters

Published by Abdo & Daughters, 4940 Viking Drive, Suite 622, Edina, Minnesota 55435.

Copyright © 1996 by Abdo Consulting Group, Inc., Pentagon Tower, P.O. Box 36036, Minneapolis, Minnesota 55435 USA. International copyrights reserved in all countries. No part of this book may be reproduced in any form without written permission from the publisher.

Printed in the United States.

Cover Photo credits: Wide World Photos / Allsport
Interior Photo credits: Wide World Photos

Edited by Paul Joseph

Library of Congress Cataloging-in-Publication Data

Italia, Bob, 1955—
        The Carolina Panthers / Bob Italia.
                p.   cm. -- (Inside the NFL)
        Includes index.
        Summary: Examines the two teams which began play in 1995, focusing on the makeup of and prospects for the new team in North Carolina.
        ISBN 1-56239-534-3
        1. Carolina Panthers (Football team)--History--Juvenile literature. 2. National Football League--History--Juvenile literature. [1. Carolina Panthers (Football team)] I. Title. II. Series: Italia, Bob, 1955— Inside the NFL.
        GV956.C27I83   1996
        796.332'64'09756--dc20   95-43590
                                                                        CIP
                                                                        AC

CONTENTS

Not Just Another Expansion Team

Unlike the Tampa Bay Buccaneers, who lost their first 26 games in 1976-77, the Carolina Panthers resembled a National Football League (NFL) team from the start. Carolina had four victories midway through its rookie season. Their amazing victory over the defending Super Bowl Champion San Francisco 49ers at Candlestick Park set a record for victories by an expansion franchise.

"I guess everyone would have been a little surprised, but they have twice the resources those other teams had," said New England coach Bill Parcells, whose Patriots lost to Carolina. "The league wanted it that way. The league wanted these teams to be better, and it's good for the game that they are."

Free agency gave the newest expansion teams a big jump on the competition, but the NFL also chipped in with extra draft picks. They also provided Carolina with a

Head coach Dom Capers and Lamar Lathon after a victory.

**Opposite page:
Vince Workman (34) and Mark Dennis celebrate a touchdown.**

generous expansion draft made up of unprotected veteran players from existing NFL teams.

"If you were ever going to buy a new team and get started, this last year was the year to do it," San Francisco 49ers coach George Seifert said. "The organizations that put the teams together did excellent jobs. You could follow it and say, 'Oh, man, these guys are going to have pretty good football teams.'"

Maybe Carolina and Jacksonville deserved to be better than their predecessors. They paid $140 million apiece for the right to become the NFL's 29th and 30th teams. Tampa Bay and Seattle paid $16 million. Either way, the Panthers received two first-round picks each in the 1995 college draft compared to one each for Tampa Bay and Seattle in 1976.

But the biggest difference was free agency. Carolina's roster consisted of 31 free agents, 13 veterans who were left unprotected by other teams in the expansion draft, 7 rookies selected in the college draft, and 2 players who were waived by their teams.

"You can't look at these kind of teams as expansion teams," said 49ers center Jesse Sapolu. "This is the age of free agency. You look at the Tampa Bay rosters and the Seattle rosters from the first few years, they didn't have a Sam Mills or a Pete Metzelaars."

Mills, a four-time Pro Bowl linebacker with the New Orleans Saints, was the leader of a Carolina defense that started just one rookie. Metzelaars was the starting tight end on Buffalo's Super Bowl teams. While Jacksonville chose to build with younger players, Carolina relied heavily on free agents.

"It was a big part of our plan to attempt to bring in veteran free agents we knew some things about," said Carolina coach Dom Capers. "We wanted guys who could be leaders because we didn't have any illusions that we were going to jump out and be 5-0."

"As it ended up," he continued, "we started 0-5. I think it's important to get the right type of veteran players who know that it takes hard work to get better. Those guys enabled us to hang in there and continue to work, and that enabled us to win the last three games."

Carolina did not sign high-priced players in the expansion draft. The only million-dollar salary the Panthers paid was to former Tampa Bay and Cleveland receiver Mark Carrier. Even after paying top draft pick Kerry Collins a $7 million signing bonus, Carolina was nearly $6 million under the salary cap—the league limit for the total amount a team can pay all of its players.

In just their first year, Carolina was talking about the playoffs. With more draft picks on the way, they seemed like a sure bet to reach their goal.

Linebacker Sam Mills (51) tackles Robert Green (22) of the Bears.

Beginnings

On October 26, 1993, the NFL Expansion Committee decided that a professional football team in the Carolinas was a good idea for the NFL. Carolina was chosen first over several other locations in the United States to receive one of the two expansion teams planned, bringing the number of NFL teams from 28 to 30.

The Carolina Panthers, along with the Jaguars in Jacksonville, Florida, were the first expansion teams since the Tampa Bay Buccaneers and the Seattle Seahawks joined the league in the mid-1970s. The Panthers were based in Charlotte, North Carolina.

A group of investors led by Jerry and Mark Richardson of Spartanburg, South Carolina, pitched together to push for the NFL expansion franchise.

Jerry Richardson was a former player with the Baltimore Colts. He caught a touchdown pass in the 1959 NFL championship game against the New York Giants. After he quit the league, Richardson returned to Spartanburg where he started his restaurant empire with one of the first Hardee's franchises.

Mike McCormack, another former NFL player and former head coach, was the team president. Bill Polian, former general manager of the Bills, now became the Panthers general manager.

Opposite page:
Linebacker Darion Conner (56) helps in bringing down a Tampa Bay running back.

The Coach

Dom Capers signed on as the head coach of the Panthers. He had been the secondary coach under Jim Mora at New Orleans before Pittsburgh Steelers' head coach Bill Cowher hired him as defensive coordinator in 1992. Under Capers, the Steelers' defense ranked second only to Dallas in the NFL and led the league in sacks with 55. The Steelers also allowed the second-fewest points in the NFL.

The Panthers were fined $150,000 and two draft picks in the first week of 1995 for attempting to negotiate with Capers. The Steelers were in the first week of the playoff season, preparing to host the Cleveland Browns. The *Pittsburgh Post-Gazette* suddenly announced that the 44-year-old Capers had agreed to become the Panthers first head coach. The NFL has a ruling, forbidding teams from talking to coaches, or players, while they are still on active teams during the season.

After the Steelers loss to the San Diego Chargers, Capers signed on. The Panthers general manager and president filled several key coaching positions while finalizing Capers' contract.

Capers began coaching as a graduate assistant at Kent State in 1972 after graduating from Mount Union College. From there, he coached at Washington, Hawaii, San Jose State, California, Tennessee and Ohio State. Then he joined Jim Mora with the United States Football League (USFL) Philadelphia-Baltimore Stars in 1984.

**Opposite page:
Head coach Dom Capers smiles as he runs off the field after their first victory.**

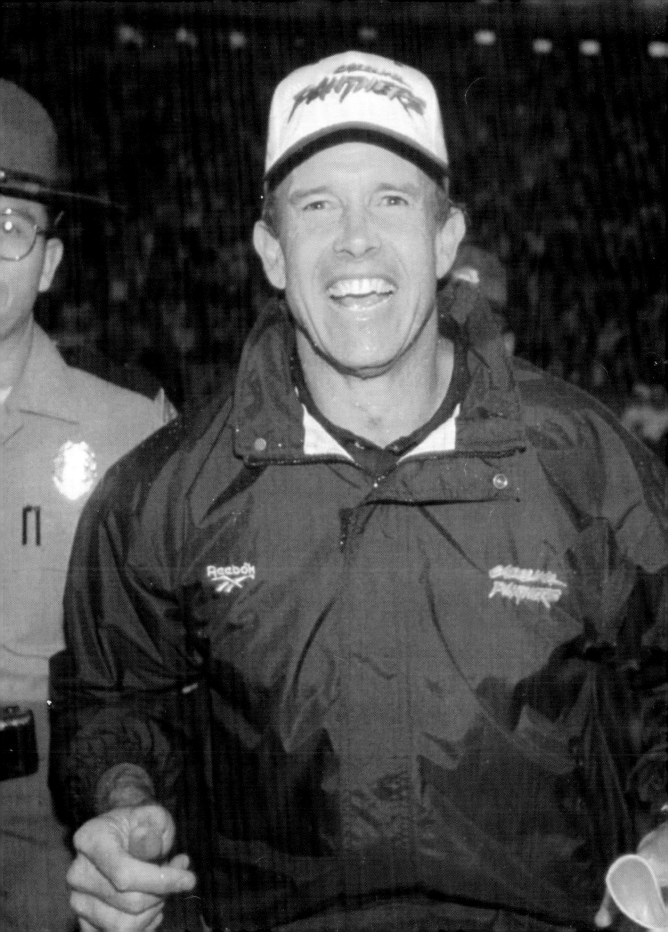

Home Sweet Home

The Panthers would play in Carolinas Stadium, which in 1996 was under construction. The stadium would seat about 72,000 fans and would resemble Joe Robbie Stadium, home of the Miami Dolphins. It was scheduled to open for the 1996 NFL season.

Until Carolinas Stadium was completed, home games were played in Clemson, South Carolina, at Frank Howard Memorial Stadium.

Training camp, which runs from mid-July to the end of August, would be held at Wofford College in Spartanburg starting in summer 1995 and continuing each summer. Once the Panthers "broke camp" after their final exhibition season game in August, they would hold their daily practice sessions at Winthrop College in Rock Hill, South Carolina. They would continue to practice at Winthrop all season long.

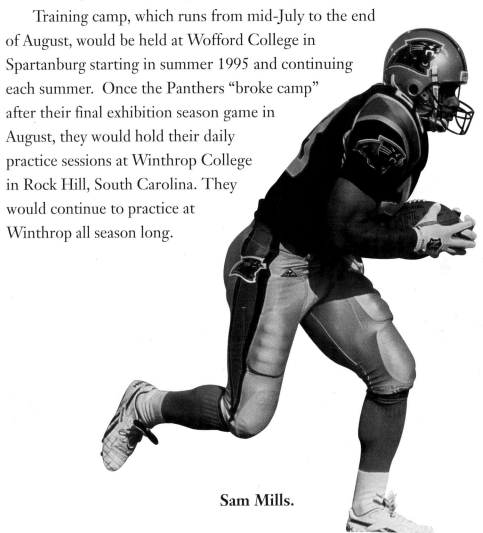

Sam Mills.

First Players Sign Up

The Panthers signed their first ten players on December 15, 1994. These were free agents who were not active with any team at that time. They were wide receivers Willie Green and Eric Weir, running backs Tony Smith and Randy Cuthbert, tackles Kevin Farkas and Mike Finn, guards Carlson Leomiti and Darryl Moore, and tight ends Lawyer Tillman and Matthew Campbell.

The Panthers stocked their roster with 35 players from other NFL clubs in February in a veteran player allocation draft held in New York. According to league rules, the Panthers had to select at least 30 players in the draft but no more than 42.

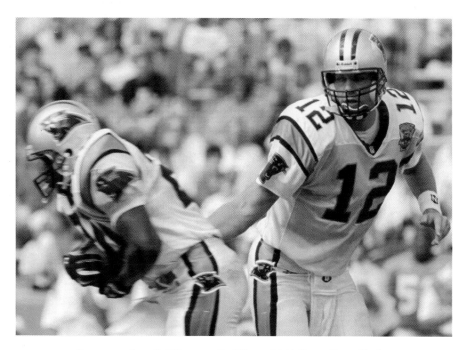

Quarterback Kerry Collins (12) hands off the ball to running back Derrick Moore.

Each of the 28 existing NFL clubs had to make 6 qualified players available from their 1994 final roster. These players could not be punters or kickers and would be physically able to play when the 1995 preseason training camps began in July.

To qualify for the expansion draft, a player had to have an NFL contract for the 1995 season. Players without 1995 contracts also qualified for the expansion draft, but only if they were free agents.

The Panthers roster ranged from high-priced free agents to castoffs to promising rookies. And they covered a wide range of ages.

Thirty-six-year-old linebacker Sam Mills, a four-time Pro Bowl selection, was the Panthers' defensive leader. Kerry Collins and fellow first-round draft choice Tyrone Poole headed the offense.

The 22-year-old Collins was the youngest starting quarterback in the NFL. He quickly established himself as a confident leader.

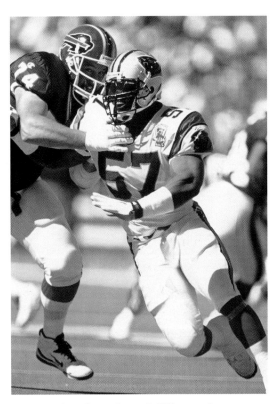

Linebacker Sam Mills rushes the passer.

When Poole first arrived from Fort Valley State, reporters marveled about how the cornerback had almost no body fat on his 5-foot-8, 185-pound frame. Two days after the start of training camp, they raved about his hard hitting and incredible speed.

Training Camp

Jerry Richardson's connection with Wofford College was strong. He credited the small college in Spartanburg for much of his success in life.

"I don't want this to sound too dramatic," said Richardson, "but if it were not for Wofford College, I would never have met my wife Rosalind. We would not have our three precious children, and the NFL would not be in the Carolinas."

In the 1950s, Richardson first came to Wofford with the help of Bob Prevatte, assistant coach of Fayetteville High School. Prevatte liked Richardson's attitude, intelligence, determination and competitiveness. He drove Richardson to the Wofford campus for an interview with Conley Snidow, Wofford's head coach. Snidow arranged a $250 scholarship for Richardson towards the $800 tuition.

Richardson made the most of the opportunity. He twice made the Little College All-American team, the NAIA All-America team, and three times the South Carolina All State. Some of the records he set at Wofford still stand.

After his graduation, Richardson played for the Baltimore Colts. In 1959, he was the Colts Rookie of the Year. In the NFL championship game, he caught a pass from Johnny Unitas, which helped seal the 31-16 win over the New York Giants.

After his NFL career, Richardson returned to Spartanburg. With Wofford teammate Charlie Bradshaw, he bought the first Hardee's franchise and eventually built Spartan Foods.

Over the years, he worked hard to bring professional football to the Carolinas. When the time finally arrived, Richardson did not forget the college that helped his own career. Wofford became the home of the Carolina Panthers' Summer Training Facility, giving his college national recognition.

**Running back Derrick Moore reacts
after the Panthers score a touchdown.**

The First Game

The Panthers played their first game against the Jacksonville Jaguars in the 1995 Hall of Fame Game in Canton, Ohio. Each year, the preseason game was played on Hall of Fame Weekend, when the current enshrinees were inducted into the Pro Football Hall of Fame. The Panthers defeated the Jaguars 20-14.

The 1995 Hall of Fame enshrinement ceremonies shared top billing with the opening of the inaugural season for these two new NFL teams. The Panthers and the Jaguars, after almost two years of preparation, took the field before a record Hall of Fame Game crowd of 24,625 fans. For the first time ever, the game had its own logo and its own slogan, "The Tradition Begins."

It was the first time in history that two expansion teams faced each other in their first game. Fawcet Field, across the street from the Hall of Fame, had temporary stands set up to accommodate an extra 773 spectators—the largest crowd in Hall of Fame history.

Because of the unique matchup, the game attracted more interest than any other game in the series that began in 1962. Since 1971, the game has matched an AFC team against an NFC team.

With the win, the NFC held a 14-10 edge in the series. The 1980 contest between the Green Bay Packers and the San Diego Chargers ended in a 0-0 tie.

The Panthers finished the preseason with a surprising 3-2 record. But now, playtime was over. The regular season was upon them—and they were about to play the NFL's frontline players for the rest of the season.

CAROLINA PANTHERS

Head coach Dom Capers.

20   30   40

Quarterback Kerry Collins.

CAR
PANT

Linebacker Darion Conner.

20   30   40

40   10

Running back Derrick Moore.

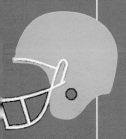

Wide receiver Eric Guliford.

40   30   20

**Running back
Howard Griffith.**

CAROLINA
PANTHERS

The First Regular-Season Game

The Atlanta Falcons hosted the Panthers at the Georgia Dome in Atlanta, Georgia, for the 1995 season opener. The Panthers led through much of the first half, building a 13-3 lead, but the Falcons made adjustments and came back in the second half. They built a 20-13 lead after Frank Reich was intercepted.

The Carolina Panthers forced overtime and nearly became the second expansion team ever to win its opener before Morten Andersen kicked a 35-yard field goal to give the Atlanta Falcons a 23-20 victory.

Trailing 20-13, Carolina started its game-tying drive at its own 20-yard line with 1:15 left in regulation. Frank Reich immediately threw a 23-yard pass to running back Bob Christian, who raced out of bounds. After two incompletions, Reich connected with Willie Green on a 13-yard pass to the Atlanta 44-yard line with 26 seconds left.

Reich then dropped back and found Green, who juggled the ball but came down with it in the end zone with 26 seconds to go. The Panthers lined up for the two-point conversion but were penalized for illegal procedure, forcing coach Dom Capers to go for the extra point.

But in overtime, Reich fumbled attempting to pass on the first possession as Lester Archambeau knocked the ball loose and recovered it at the Carolina 31-yard line, setting up the game-winning field goal. While losing the game, the Panthers showed that they came to play with the big boys.

**Opposite page:
Eric Guliford (84) returns
a punt for a touchdown.**

The First Regular-Season Home Game

The Panthers hosted the St. Louis Rams as their first regular season home opponent in Week 3 of the 1995 season. The Rams dominated the game, forcing seven turnovers and capitalizing on four of them for scores, for a 31-10 rout. All three quarterbacks for the Panthers were ineffective.

"What you saw out there today was a Carolina team that played sloppy against a good football team," said Capers. "The Rams have an excellent football team. They did a good job taking the ball away. We turned the ball over seven times and for us to have a chance to win the game, we had to protect the football."

Carolina starter Frank Reich was 8-of-19 for 68 yards and an interception, while backup Jack Trudeau was 11-for-17 for 100 yards and 3 interceptions and rookie Kerry Collins completed 7-of-11 passes for 45 yards and an interception.

John Kasay got the Panthers on the board with a 45-yard field goal as the first half ended, but Parker scooped up a Willie Green fumble and raced down the left sidelines for a touchdown midway through the third quarter to extend the St. Louis lead to 21-3.

A Todd Lyght interception set up Steve McLaughlin's 34-yard field goal before Dorn scored to make it 31-3 with just over five minutes remaining in the game.

Collins scored the Panthers' only touchdown on a 1-yard plunge with 1:57 left. A crowd of 54,060 attended the game.

After a bye in Week 4, the Panthers played the Tampa Bay Buccaneers. Backup quarterback Casey Weldon's 1-yard touchdown dive on the first play of the fourth quarter allowed Tampa Bay to keep the Panthers winless with a 20-13 victory.

Quarterback Kerry Collins (12) passes the ball.

The Panthers fell to 0-4 and were struggling for offense, scoring just 32 points over their last 3 games. The Panthers had a chance to tie the game, but their drive ended on downs at the Tampa Bay 22-yard line with 1:05 remaining. Carolina had four turnovers, all in Tampa Bay territory.

The frustration continued the following week in Chicago. Robert Green's 1-yard touchdown run with 27 seconds remaining gave the Chicago Bears a 31-27 win over the Panthers, who nearly recorded their first win in a back-and-forth contest.

Eric Guliford's 62-yard punt return for a touchdown gave Carolina a 27-24 lead with 2:37 left. Guliford, a little-used third-year receiver from Arizona State, fielded the punt near the right sideline, cut toward the middle of the field then back to the right sideline, where he dashed untouched for the go-ahead score. With the loss, Carolina fell to 0-5.

The First Regular-Season Victory

The Panthers recorded the first win in franchise history as John Kasay kicked four field goals in a 26-15 victory over the New York Jets.

The Panthers (1-5) trailed 12-3 late in the first half, but reeled off 20 straight points to build a 23-12 lead. Kasay kicked his second field goal of the game with just over two minutes left in the first half to cut the deficit to 12-6. A 20-yard pass from Kerry Collins to Eric Guilford on third-and-fourteen kept the drive alive.

In Week 8, the Panthers hosted the New Orleans Saints. Howard Griffith ran for one touchdown and caught another in the third quarter as the Panthers won their second straight game, 20-3 over the New Orleans Saints. The 2-5 Panthers snapped a 3-3 halftime tie and became the first team to hold the Saints without a touchdown in the 1995 season.

Brett Maxie intercepted a pass by Jim Everett and returned it to the New Orleans 23-yard line to set up the first score. Kerry Collins connected with Mark Carrier for 12 yards and Derrick Moore ran 9 yards to the 2-yard line. Griffith then dove in for his first touchdown of the season with 7:39 remaining in the quarter.

On the Saints' next possession, Bubba McDowell picked off Everett and returned it to the New Orleans 20-yard line. Four plays later, Collins hit Griffith on a 1-yard swing pass for a 17-3 lead. John Kasay capped the scoring in the fourth quarter with a 37-yard field goal, his sixth in the last two games. The kick finished a 67-yard drive in which Moore gained 42 yards on the ground.

Panther Brett Maxie (39) stops receiver Michael Haynes (81).

Week 9 saw the Panthers streak hit three-in-a-row—this time against the New England Patriots. It was the first time in NFL history that an expansion team had won three games in a row. John Kasay's 29-yard field goal with 7:52 remaining in overtime earned the victory.

The Panthers won the coin toss in overtime and drove to the New England 37. Capers elected to punt rather than try a long field goal or go for it on fourth-and-four. The decision paid off, as the punt pinned the Patriots at their own nine-yard line. New England gained only one yard in three plays and the struggling Pat O'Neill had to punt from his own end zone, giving Carolina possession at the Patriots 32-yard line.

Derrick Moore gained 20 yards on 4 carries, leading to Kasay's winning kick. Moore carried 28 times for 119 yards.

Kerry Collins drove the Panthers down the field in the final seconds, but Kasay's 39-yard field goal attempt with 4 seconds remaining hit the left upright and bounced away.

A Super Upset

In Week 10, the Panthers made history again by beating Super Bowl Champion San Francisco 49ers on their own field. Veteran cornerback Tim McKyer returned an interception 96 yards for a touchdown and John Kasay kicked a pair of field goals in the first half to lead the Panthers to their stunning 13-7 victory.

The win was the fourth in a row for the 4-5 Panthers, who tied a record for most wins by a first-year expansion team shared by Minnesota, Atlanta, Miami, New Orleans and Cincinnati.

Back home, Carolina broadcasters cheered the arrival of the good news. The Charlotte Observer devoted a front-page story to the Panthers' victory and topped it off with a headline that screamed "Unbelievable!" Inside, the newspaper even suggested the possibility of the expansion team qualifying for the postseason.

At the Panthers' temporary training complex in nearby Rock Hill, South Carolina, Polian chuckled at the interest generated by the team's four-game winning streak after an 0-5 start. He liked what he had seen so far, but he was quick to point out that the team still had a lot of work to do.

"You can see the blueprint of a pretty good team emerging through the mist," he said, "if we can continue to add personnel and make big plays."

The streak came to an end, November 12, in St. Louis, at the Rams opening game in their new home, the Trans World Dome. Chris Miller threw two touchdown passes and Jerome Bettis ran for a score as St. Louis won 28-17.

A Tale of Two Seasons

For now, those within the organization are avoiding the hype and hysteria of making the playoffs. There are too many things that can go wrong—like the injury of a key player.

In addition, the people in Carolina's front office can still recall the days of January, when you didn't need a program to tell who the Panthers were because there weren't enough of them.

"It is not, in our view, a benchmark win," Polian said of the win over the 49ers. "There's still a long way to go in our season and a long way to go in our development. I suspect that at the end of the season, we'll find that there's still a lot of work to be done. I don't suspect. I know."

Capers calls it the tale of two seasons. First his expansion team learned how to deal with adversity. Now it's learning how to handle success.

"The challenges continue to change for us each week,"

Defenseman Carlton Bailey sacks Jets quarterback Bubby Brister.

Capers said as he reviewed the Panthers victory over San Francisco.

One month ago, Capers was talking about how the Panthers could right themselves after an 0-5 start. After the victory over the

Running back Howard Griffith.

defending Super Bowl champions, and Capers was being asked about playoff possibilities.

"We haven't even reached the .500 point yet," he said, "and there's no way I can look anybody in the eye and even think about playoffs if we aren't even a .500 football team."

You can write to the Carolina Panthers at the following address:

The Carolina Panthers Football Club
227 W. Trade St.
Charlotte, NC 28202

Include a self-addressed stamped envelope if you want a reply.

GLOSSARY

ALL-PRO—A player who is voted to the Pro Bowl.

BACKFIELD—Players whose position is behind the line of scrimmage.

CORNERBACK—Either of two defensive halfbacks stationed a short distance behind the linebackers and relatively near the sidelines.

DEFENSIVE END—A defensive player who plays on the end of the line and often next to the defensive tackle.

DEFENSIVE TACKLE—A defensive player who plays on the line and between the guard and end.

ELIGIBLE—A player who is qualified to be voted into the Hall of Fame.

END ZONE—The area on either end of a football field where players score touchdowns.

EXTRA POINT—The additional one-point score added after a player makes a touchdown. Teams earn extra points if the placekicker kicks the ball through the uprights of the goalpost, or if an offensive player crosses the goal line with the football before being tackled.

FIELD GOAL—A three-point score awarded when a placekicker kicks the ball through the uprights of the goalpost.

FULLBACK—An offensive player who often lines up farthest behind the front line.

FUMBLE—When a player loses control of the football.

GUARD—An offensive lineman who plays between the tackles and center.

GROUND GAME—The running game.

HALFBACK—An offensive player whose position is behind the line of scrimmage.

HALFTIME—The time period between the second and third quarters of a football game.

INTERCEPTION—When a defensive player catches a pass from an offensive player.

KICK RETURNER—An offensive player who returns kickoffs.

LINEBACKER—A defensive player whose position is behind the line of scrimmage.

LINEMAN—An offensive or defensive player who plays on the line of scrimmage.

PASS—To throw the ball.

PASS RECEIVER—An offensive player who runs pass routes and catches passes.

PLACEKICKER—An offensive player who kicks extra points and field goals. The placekicker also kicks the ball from a tee to the opponent after his team has scored.

PLAYOFFS—The postseason games played amongst the division winners and wild card teams which determines the Super Bowl champion.

PRO BOWL—The postseason All-Star game which showcases the NFL's best players.

PUNT—To kick the ball to the opponent.

QUARTER—One of four 15-minute time periods that makes up a football game.

QUARTERBACK—The backfield player who usually calls the signals for the plays.

REGULAR SEASON—The games played after the preseason and before the playoffs.

ROOKIE—A first-year player.

RUNNING BACK—A backfield player who usually runs with the ball.

RUSH—To run with the football.

SACK—To tackle the quarterback behind the line of scrimmage.

SAFETY—A defensive back who plays behind the linemen and linebackers. Also, two points awarded for tackling an offensive player in his own end zone when he's carrying the ball.

SPECIAL TEAMS—Squads of football players that perform special tasks (for example, kickoff team and punt-return team).

SPONSOR—A person or company that finances a football team.

SUPER BOWL—The NFL Championship game played between the AFC champion and the NFC champion.

T FORMATION—An offensive formation in which the fullback lines up behind the center and quarterback with one halfback stationed on each side of the fullback.

TACKLE—An offensive or defensive lineman who plays between the ends and the guards.

TAILBACK—The offensive back farthest from the line of scrimmage.

TIGHT END—An offensive lineman who is stationed next to the tackles, and who usually blocks or catches passes.

TOUCHDOWN—When one team crosses the goal line of the other team's end zone. A touchdown is worth six points.

TURNOVER—To turn the ball over to an opponent either by a fumble, an interception, or on downs.

UNDERDOG—The team that is picked to lose the game.

WIDE RECEIVER—An offensive player who is stationed relatively close to the sidelines and who usually catches passes.

WILD CARD—A team that makes the playoffs without winning its division.

ZONE PASS DEFENSE—A pass defense method where defensive backs defend a certain area of the playing field rather than individual pass receivers.

INDEX